Ma'vel

STARLIGHT MERMEN

SKYE MACKINNON

Peryton Press

Contents

The Original Legend

Jonet Forsyth lived on the Orkney island of Westray in the 17th century. In 1627, she foresaw the demise of her sweetheart Benjamin Garrioch and begged him not to go to sea, but he didn't listen. After he drowned, the islanders who were already suspicious of Jonet began to accuse her of being a witch in earnest. Things escalated when during a storm Jonet saved the crew of a ship that had got in trouble. Since nobody thought a mere woman could achieve such a feat, she was ostracised further and finally taken to stand trial in Kirkwall. She was convicted as a witch and sentenced to be strangled and burned at the stake.

All that is fact. However, legend says she was spirited away on the night before her execution by her sweetheart...

The finmen appearing in this story are a Scottish myth likely based on Inuit sailors.

"The sea is the greatest witch in all the world."
Unnamed Shetland woman, 1882

Author's Note

Dear readers,

Some events and characters in this book are based on historical events. Jonet Forsyth (sometimes known as Janet) was a real person mentioned in various books and sources from the time. All the 'crimes' Jonet supposedly committed are taken straight from the trial protocols, as are the names of those who accused her of witchcraft. As much as I would like to say that I made up some of the (ridiculous) accusations, I did not. This isn't fantasy, it's the sad reality of a very dark period of Scottish history.

Between 1590 and 1727, around 2,500 people suspected of witchcraft were executed in Scotland, most of them women. In the Orkney Islands to the north of mainland Scotland, where this story is set, at least 72 people were put to trial.

This book is dedicated to all of them.

I've included a little list of interesting books and sources at the end in case you want to delve further into the dark world of Scotland's witch hunts.

Happy reading,
  Skye MacKinnon

ORKNEY
(UNITED KINGDOM)

Prologue

In the first ye the said Jonet ar indytit and accusit for airt and pairt of the abominable superstitioun and superstitious abusing and disceveing of the people within the said Isle and for practeising of the wicked and devilish pointis of witchcraft and devilrie done by yow. In maner at the tyme and in the places efterspecefeit. And in giving yourselff furth to have sutch craft and knawledge thairof.

— TRIAL REPORT PUBLISIIED IN
'PUBLICATIONS OF THE FOLK-LORE
SOCIETY', 1878

KIRKWALL, ORKNEY ISLANDS, SCOTLAND

The judge stared at me from beneath bushy eyebrows as if he couldn't wait to see me burned at the stake.

"You stand accused," he began and the hall fell quiet, "of eighteen counts of witchcraft. Jonet Forsyth, daughter of William Forsyth of Howrnes within the isle of Westray, you will face trial in the name of God. Stand now and be judged."

I felt the weight of dozens of glares on my back as I staggered to my feet. Half of Westray seemed to have come to the Mainland to witness my trial. Some of them had never left the island, yet here they were, eager to see me burn. How could I have caused them to hate me this much? What had I ever done to them?

"You are indicted and accused for abusing and deceiving the people of Westray and for practising wicked and devilish witchcraft." The judge sounded as if he was personally affronted by my supposed offences. I'd never met him, but maybe he knew one of the islanders who'd come to speak out against me. Or maybe he was just an angry man who liked to sneer at those he deemed lesser.

"First, you are accused of slaying four pigs belonging to Manss Peitersone in Kirbuster."

"I didn't-"

The guard behind me wrapped his filthy hand around my mouth while the judge shot me another hateful glare.

He checked his notes before continuing. "When Mareoun Flet ate some of that pork, she fell gravely ill and has been decrepit for the past five years. When she confronted you with this fact, you didn't deny that you were responsible."

I wanted to tell him that Mareoun had never been quite right in the head and that it had nothing to do with eating pork – which of course hadn't been from a pig killed by me – but the guard still had his hand pressed against my mouth. Every time I breathed, I couldn't help but smell the iron scent of blood clinging to his fingers. It may have even been my own blood.

"You are furthermore accused of casting sickness upon Thomas Port six years ago in February. When his wife voiced her suspicions, you came to their house and cured him of his deadly disease. They even paid you for your service!"

The judge shouted the last bit, spittle flying from his lips. He was really taking this personal. I, on the other hand, barely remembered ever visiting the Ports. Six years was a long time ago. Maybe I had given him some of my herbs; who knew. I certainly hadn't made him sick in the first place, though.

"But that wasn't enough for you, Jonet Forsyth. You healed Thomas Port by passing on his disease to Michaell Reid's mare. The healthier Mr Port became, the sicker the horse got until it died. And when they cut open the mare, do you know what they found?"

He left the audience hanging, taking several deep breaths to prolong the dramatic pause. I just wanted him to get on with it. My legs were shaking, I could barely breathe and I hadn't slept in days. If this nonsense was going to last much longer, I'd collapse.

"They found no heart inside the mare's chest!" the judge roared to the gasps and shocked shouts of the people behind me. "There was nothing but a blob of water where her heart should have been! Witchcraft!"

"Witch!" several people hissed, their voices dripping with hate. Once again, I wondered what I'd done to them. I'd never hurt anyone. On the contrary, I'd helped many of them. At least three of the men in the kirk wouldn't be alive without me. Yet here they were, clamouring for my death.

"You are indicted and accused of going to the sea at night at midsummer six years ago. You took a can full of saltwater and through some devilish practice, you took away the profits of a local man named Johne Herkas."

"She did!" Johne shouted from the back of the kirk. I couldn't believe it. I'd known him since we were children. We'd never been close, but I'd never had any quarrel with him. Why would he accuse me of such a crime? What was he to gain from it?

I'd asked myself that question many times while waiting for my trial to begin. I didn't have much. My little croft and the meagre possessions within were all I owned. I wasn't rich. There was no money to be had after I died.

The judge continued throwing accusations at me. Poisoning livestock. Making neighbours ill. Causing storms. That one hurt the most. As if I'd ever want to drown in the sea. They seemed to have forgotten that I lost my Benjamin in a storm. Even now, after hearing all those hurtful allegations, I didn't wish anyone ill. Maybe I should have. If I'd been anything like what they suggested, I'd have made a pact with the devil to take revenge. But I wasn't. I just wanted to live my life in peace.

From the way the judge was behaving, I doubted my life would be very long. I droned out his voice and thought of better days. A time when Benjamin and I were making plans for a life together. We were happy. He'd been about to ask my father for my hand in marriage. The life I'd dreamed of had been so close – until everything went to pieces. Now I was far from home and might not live through another night. How could it all go so wrong?

By the time the judge was finally done, he was red-faced and I was close to fainting. The guard had finally taken his hand off my mouth, but I could still smell his stench, as if he hadn't bathed in months. If only I had some herbs to rub under my nose to get rid of the smell. It would give me some comfort, reminding me of home where bundles of dried herbs lined the rafters. Would they grant me one last wish, or would they drag me up to Gallow's Ha' as soon as the trial was over?

I'd not seen the place where they executed the witches, but some of the guards had talked about it. It was up the hill, looking down on Kirkwall. At least I'd die with a view. I suppressed a hysterical laugh. I wouldn't give them the satisfaction of seeing me as the crazed, vengeful woman they portrayed me as.

"Now the witnesses will speak," the judge announced. "We shall start with Robert Reid."

Bile rose in my throat. If I'd ever truly hated someone,

it was him. He'd started it all. The rumours, the whispered words behind my back. His sons had been the first to throw stones at me. He hadn't stopped them; he'd encouraged them to throw harder. If I had to guess, it had been him who'd reported me. There were few other islanders who I could imagine doing such a thing, despite all the charges brought against me today. At heart, they weren't evil people. Just misguided and scared. Ever since the first witch burned here in Kirkwall, everyone'd been looking over their shoulder. Ill omens were seen everywhere. Whenever something awful happened, it was blamed on witches. In the past, a storm was just a storm. Now, it was a witch's doing. If the islanders were to be believed, my doing.

Robert Reid stepped to the front. Stood next to the judge, I realised how similar they looked. Both had blotchy, red-veined faces that spoke of a hot temper and too much ale. Both were broad-shouldered men, although Robert had the thick arms of a sailor while the judge's stature held more fat than muscle. Having one of them glare at me with eyes sparking with hate was bad enough, but two next to each other? My knees finally gave in and I crumpled to the kirk's stone floor.

"Get up," the guard behind me snapped and tried to drag me to my feet, but my legs wouldn't comply.

When he realised I wasn't able to stand, he turned to the judge. "Shall I get her a chair?"

The judge shook his head. "Leave her on the floor." Where she belongs. He didn't say it, but he didn't have to. His sneer spoke for him.

Cold seeped into my limbs while I lay there, half

sitting, half lying. My hands were shackled in front of me, preventing me from pushing myself into a more comfortable position.

I let my mind drift to other days, other times, when I'd been a free woman and not a witch.

One

Item ye ar indyttit and accusit for devilish and abominable bewitching of Robert Reid in Coat in Gaird in casting seiknes upoun him, he being upoun the sea, in sick sort. That the men that wer in the boit with him were forcit to bring him on shore for fear of death. And ye being on the shore at his arryvall. He challengit yow for his seiknes and threitened yow In thir words: giff he gott not his health againe It sould be wors nor enough with yow Quhairupoun ye washit him with salt watter. Quhairby he recovcrit and cam to the sea In health upoun the morne.

— TRIAL REPORT PUBLISHED IN
'PUBLICATIONS OF THE FOLK-LORE
SOCIETY', 1878

"*It will be fine, love.*" *He smiled at me, already half-turning to his boat and the other sailors waiting for him. "It's a calm day. I'll be home before you know it."*

I grabbed his shirt and pulled him close, clinging to him. "Don't go. I've seen it. If you go, you'll never return." Tears burned in my eyes and my heart was still pounding with the weight of my vision. "Please, stay with me."

He gently extracted himself from my grip. Bereft of his touch, I hugged myself. Cold fog surrounded us and I was only wearing a shawl above my nightgown. I'd run to the harbour faster than I'd ever run before in the desperate hope to catch Ben before he left.

"I'll be fine," he repeated. "It was just a bad dream. Go home before you catch a cold. I'll come by when we're back and bring you some fish."

"I don't want fish," I wailed and reached out for him again. He stepped back, regret reflecting on his gorgeous face.

"See you tonight, Jonet," he said and joined the other sailors. He didn't look back.

Hot tears streamed down my face as I watched his boat sail off into the fog, knowing I'd never see him again.

I woke with the knowledge that something bad was going to happen. It made me want to pull the blanket over my head and stay in bed, but Connor the cockerel had already cried for the fourth time. He'd continue to do so every few minutes until I brought him and his brides their breakfast. That feathery beast had become way too manipulative. I should show him how easily he could end up in my next chicken soup.

While I cooked my porridge on my soot-covered stove, I tried to remember last night's dreams. Some days, I could recall even the smallest detail, but today, only the feeling of dread remained. It made me shiver. I wrapped my shawl tighter around my shoulders. Autumn was approaching quickly and the nights were getting colder. In the past, I used to look forward to winter because it meant Benjamin was home more. Now, winter was nothing but the death of warmth and light. Another shiver ran down my back and I leaned over the stove for warmth. The porridge was starting to grow thick and gooey, almost ready to eat. I licked my lips. The warm meal would hopefully push away this dark mood. I had a busy day ahead and couldn't linger on the past nor on my dreams.

The wind pulled on my hair while I fed the chickens and checked on the sheep. Most of them were strewn all across the island, only to return to my croft for shearing, but at the moment, I had two poorly ewes in the barn. They weren't happy about being locked indoors, but I didn't have time to repair the fence of the small enclosure beside the house. I had so many more important things to deal with than a broken fence, although I made a mental note to ask Mary if her husband could come and fix it for me. I knew she had trouble paying for the ointment I made her every week, even though I charged her less than I would anyone else, so maybe she'd agree to the trade.

Before, such a thing would have been normal. Among islanders, using money wasn't all that common. We bartered and traded goods, knowledge and our time. Everyone else still did so, but me...

Again, I forced myself to dispel the shadows of the past. It was turning out to be one of those days. Every time I thought I'd become used to everything that happened, my heart sharply reminded me that it wasn't done grieving. Maybe I never would be. I hadn't just lost Ben. I'd lost everything.

With the chickens and ewes taken care of, I grabbed my satchel. If I hurried, I might get to Pierowall before the clouds would start to empty their load. They hung low, swallowing the top of Fitty Hill, the island's highest point. You couldn't really call it a summit. I'd been up there as a child, feeling like a true explorer, before realising when I got older that anyone who'd ever seen a real mountain would scoff at our little Fitty Hill.

Just like every time I walked to Pierowall, I regretted how far away my croft was from the island's main village. Legend had it that the Vikings had settled here many, many hundred years ago. It was a likely story. The fishermen called the bay where Pierowall now stood Orkney's best natural harbour. It protected their ships from the angry waves of the ocean, keeping them safe even on stormy days like today was going to be. My father had lived in the village until his death last year, but his house wouldn't last another winter. It would have taken more money to restore it than I could ever hope to have, so I'd sold the house and remained in my little cottage on the West side of the island.

I wrapped my fingers around the bone pendant I always wore around my neck. My father had given me the bone when I'd left home, for luck. It hadn't worked, but it reminded me of him. He'd been a good, decent man and I was glad he didn't know what I'd become since his death. What the people of Westray had made me.

By the time the village of Pierowall finally came into view, the first raindrops had started to fall. I wrapped my shawl around my head and tucked my curls underneath. They wouldn't stay under there for long. My mother had always called my hair as unruly as myself. I smiled at the memory. She hadn't been wrong. Trouble tended to find me no matter how hard I tried to avoid it. Ben's face flashed in my mind and my smile disappeared.

I tripped, just about catching myself before I could end up sprawled out on the muddy grass. *Focus, Janet. Get your head out of the clouds.* I could hear my mother's voice in my mind, as clear as if she was truly talking to me.

What was going on with me today? I seemed to be surrounded by the ghosts of the past. Ben was always there, always lurking at the back of my mind, but I didn't think about my parents all that often.

Today was different. That ominous feeling still had a grip on my heart. Something bad was going to happen and it would very likely involve me. I'd learned to trust my intuition. If Ben had believed in my premonitions the way I did, he would still be alive. Still here with me.

Oh Ben, why didn't you believe me?

A large raindrop landed on my nose, pulling me from my thoughts. I'd reached the first house and grimaced when I saw the large man working in the little garden outside. Robert Reid. The same Robert Reid who I'd thrown a bucket of water at three days ago.

He was bent over, looking at something on the other side of the stone wall. I tried to walk as quietly as possible, not wanting to attract his attention. Robert Reid was known to have a temper. I still didn't know what had possessed me to throw that bucket at him. It hadn't be the first time someone had called me a witch. I should be used to it by now.

I'd been at the harbour when his boat had come in. One of the other fishermen had been supporting Robert, whose face had been white as ewe's milk. As soon as he'd set eyes on me, he'd roared in anger. The other fishermen had to hold him back, or he would have attacked me. Even weakened by illness, he could have easily hurt me or worse if they hadn't restrained him.

He'd shouted something about me making him sick, about how all witches should be burned alive. Usually, I would have ignored him. I was used to comments like that. The entire village – no, the entire population of Westray – was convinced I was a witch. Nothing new there. But Robert Reid had been the final drop in the barrel. Without thinking, I'd grabbed a bucket someone had left next to a pile of nets and thrown it at the fisherman, only then realising that it was full of sea water.

"You," the man in question barked and I swirled around. I'd been spotted. I threw a hopeful glance at the cottage behind him, hoping his wife was in. Maybe she would stop him if he decided to attack me. Liliann had been a friend once, many years ago.

"You healed me!" Robert Reid spat.

I blinked at him, not quite understanding what he was saying. They usually accused me of poisoning their crops, causing storms or making the cattle sick. Nobody had ever accused me of healing them before.

"You're...you're welcome?" I said before I could stop and think. My mouth had always been faster than my brain and this was one of those unfortunate moments when I wished it was the other way round.

"You admit it!" he roared, something like a smirk appearing on his podgy face. "Liliann, did you hear that? The witch admitted that she healed me. I was right!"

To my relief, Liliann didn't join her husband outside. Maybe she was away. I really hoped she was.

"How did you do it?" Robert Reid asked although it didn't sound like he was particularly interested in my answer. "Did you put a spell on the water in the bucket? Or did you sneak into my house at night?"

He was raging mad. Unfortunately, he was well respected and people listened to his opinions. Once he spread this news, life would become even harder for me.

"I didn't heal you and I didn't make you sick," started, but when his eyes bulged, I stopped. He couldn't be reasoned with.

"Have a good day," I forced myself to say and hurried down the path as quickly as I could. I had a few hours before the entire village would know that I'd supposedly healed that obnoxious man. By tomorrow, everyone on the island would have heard the rumour.

My intuition had been right. Today was going to be bad.

The boat from Kirkwall had already arrived, moored at the main pier on the North edge of Pierowall. Men were carrying crates back and forth, unloading the goods the Mainlanders had brought for us and loading the boat with freshly caught fish, woven tweed and other things that we were sending back to Kirkwall in return. Westray was one of many of the Orkney islands and there was much trade between all of them. Long ago, if you believed the stories, Orkney had been the centre of the Viking trade, its ships reaching all the corners of the world. I had a hard time imagining that.

A small queue had formed on the quay, mostly locals wanting to sell their wares to the traders. Usually, I'd be one of them, but today, I wanted to buy something. I just hoped I didn't make the trip to Pierowall for nothing.

I joined the queue behind Maryanne, an elderly woman who'd been a friend of my grandmother.

"Good morning," I said politely. When she turned around, her smile turned into a frown.

"You."

I cringed under her disapproving stare. What had I done now? I hadn't even talked to Maryanne in years.

"How are you doing?" I asked, ignoring her rudeness. Treat others how you would like to be treated; that's what my mum used to say.

She didn't reply and pointedly turned around, leaving me staring at her back. Her shoulders were slumped with age and I was surprised she didn't use a walking stick despite her obvious frailness. In other circumstances, I would have recommended her some herbal teas that could help with the pains and aches of old age, but not after the way she'd greeted me.

You. Her word echoed in my mind. Was that what I'd become? Reduced to a simple *you*?

I wanted to go home. This plus the encounter with Robert Reid proved how I didn't belong here. Westray no longer felt like the island I'd grown up on, the place I'd been happy on. I tried to think back to the years before Benjamin died. If I took him out of the equation, had I been content? No, even back then there'd been stares and whispered words. Being with him had lessened them somewhat - he'd been a well-respected fisherman from a good family - but I'd already been an outcast even then. I just hadn't realised. Or maybe I didn't want to see it. Benjamin had been everything to me. Now that he was gone, my shield had disappeared. I was bare before them, vulnerable to their suspicions and hatred.

"Morning," someone muttered from behind me and I gingerly turned around, almost expecting yet another disappointment.

Bright green eyes, puffy cheeks, a gentle smile. Caitlin Roberts. What she didn't have in intelligence she made up for in kindness.

"Good morning," I said, returning her smile. It felt good to see someone who didn't seem to care who I was or what people said about me. "What are you doing here?"

"My ma wants some spices and salt. She's not well enough to come here herself so she sent me instead."

"I'm sorry to hear that," I said, meaning every word. I didn't know Caitlin's mother well, but she'd always greeted me warmly when I'd seen her.

"She's getting old," Caitlin said simply. "But is it true that you know about healing? Could you maybe-"

"Silly girl," Maryanne snapped, suddenly by my side. "Don't do business with the witch."

I wanted to say something, defend myself, tell her that I wasn't a witch, but my throat was suddenly dry and no words would come.

"I don't believe in witches," Caitlin replied to my surprise. I hadn't put her down as someone answering back to her elders, especially someone as old and well-known as Maryanne.

"Then you're even more of a fool than I thought."

Maryanne sniffed derisively and turned around again. Thank God.

I gave Caitlin a weak smile, but she didn't say anything. Was she changing her mind about me? Would she say something hurtful? Tears were threatening to burst to the surface. With one last look at the trading ship, I left the queue and fled.

Two

The islanders stood aghast at the hardihood of the Storm Witch. It was believed that nothing human could live in such a gale, even if the boat had been the best belonging to the island, which it was not.

— AROUND THE ORKNEY PEAT-
FIRES, W.R. MACINTOSH, 1914

By the time I reached the beach, the wind had picked up, turning from a breeze into the beginnings of a storm. The cold bit through my shawl and I wished I'd taken my winter coat instead. Shivers ran down my back, but it wasn't just because of the freezing wind. That bad feeling I'd woken up with was back in force. Something awful was about to happen, I knew it. But what?

A group of people stood at the other end of the sandy beach, too far away to see clearly. They were simply standing around without going about their work. How strange. They should be making sure that everything was ready to withstand the storm, that anything that could be carried away by the wind was secured. We were used to storms here and everyone knew what needed to be done. I cringed when I remembered the beating I'd received as a young girl when I'd not brought in my father's fishing net as instructed. It had been blown away and got tangled in the brush. By the time we found it the following day, it had been full of holes and tears. I'd learnt my lesson, just like everyone else. That's what made seeing these people aimlessly milling about so curious.

I hastened my step, both curiosity and dread pushing me on.

I had to lean against the wind as I made my way to the little group. The sand seemed to want to swallow up my feet, reminding me of the waves that swallowed my Benjamin. The ocean was turning into a churning monster, whipped up by the storm. Foam danced across the waves, bits of it swirling in the air.

Their voices were carried to me on the wind before I could see the men's faces. Five fishermen, three from my little village, the others from further away. I knew them all. When Benjamin had started courting me, he'd introduced me to his friends, all of them seamen. Most of them hadn't been very interested in me, but I'd spent time with them for Ben's sake.

"They're lost," Tom shouted to be heard over the noise of the strengthening storm.

"We have to do something!" That was Malcolm, one of Benjamin's best friends. He might have been best man at our wedding. That thought made the chill even worse.

"There's nothing to be done, son. They're gone. We should go home and light a candle."

They all noticed me at the same time, turning to me as one. Malcolm was the only one who didn't sneer while the others all looked like they wanted to toss me into the sea. One of them, I thought his name is Jonathan, made the sign of the cross. I almost laughed. I somehow doubted that a real witch would be affected by that.

"What's going on?" I shouted.

The men exchanged a look that turned my blood to ice.

"The *Starlight*," Malcolm said without further explanation, his voice grave. He didn't need to say more. While I didn't recognise the name, it wasn't the first ship that hadn't come home from the sea. In this storm, any ship not close to the harbour was as good as lost.

He pointed into the distance and I gasped when I saw a tiny brown dot bop up and down the waves. The *Starlight* wasn't as far away as I'd thought, but they were getting precariously close to the cliffs. Razor-sharp rocks hid beneath the surface, threatening to rip open the hull of any ship that dares to come close. The boat wasn't one of the local ones. They wouldn't know what dangers lurked there. A local could have maybe guided them out of those precarious waters and into the safety of the bay, but the five men in front of me seemed to have no intention of helping the *Starlight's* crew.

Light a candle, Tom had said. As if that would comfort the poor families about to lose their loved ones. My boat wasn't far from here. I wasn't a fisherman, but I knew the waters well enough.

They shouted after me, but I ignored them. If they didn't want to help, then I would do it myself. And if I perished while attempting to save the men from drowning, then so be it. There was nothing for me to live for.

The wind pushed me back, fighting me every step of the way, but I pressed on. Men's lives were at stake. Men like Ben. My muscles ached as I leaned against the wind. It was the kind of storm that would easily push you over if you didn't keep your balance. And it was still growing stronger. I only had a short window of time to get my boat out of its little shelter and sail to the *Starlight*.

My skiff was in the noost where I'd drawn it onto the shore, safe from the elements. The noost, a boat shaped shelter, hadn't been built by me. It and the ones next to it had been here for generations, built by long-forgotten ancestors. Maybe even the Vikings.

I needed their courage and strength.

I felt the men watching me as I pulled my boat across the beach, straining against the wind. None of them came to help. They likely wouldn't mourn me if I perished in the sea today. On the contrary, it would mean they had one less witch to deal with. I scoffed. Maybe they'd remember me more kindly once I was dead. But if I succeeded... I may have hammered the final nail into my coffin.

My premonition had been right. Today was a bad day.

The ocean welcomed me by drenching me in icy water before I'd even got into my boat. I gasped, trying to push the cold away. I had to be strong.

Benjamin needed me to do this. Maybe if I saved these men, I could forgive myself for letting him sail to his death.

The wind was too strong for the sail, so I used the oars, my muscles straining with every stroke. It felt impossible to fight the waves threatening to push me back onto the shore, but I prevailed.

Help me, God. If you're there, help me. Not for my sake. For them.

The sky was darkening, black clouds racing across, torn apart by the wind. I looked back, but the waves were too high to see the beach. I imagined them standing there, watching me. Would they say a prayer if I drowned? Would they light a candle like people did for the victims of the sea?

Probably not. That thought spurned me on further. I'd show them. I'd prove that I only wanted to help people. I'd never hurt anyone. I wasn't cursing the villagers, making them sick. It was the furthest thing from my ambitions. I just wanted to be *good*.

Slowly, the *Starlight* came into view. It was still floating, but from the way dark shapes were frantically moving on its decks, they knew they were in trouble. It was hard to see but if I was right, they were too close to one particularly sharp rock hidden just beneath the surface. In low tide, it was visible but now it was a veiled dagger about to strike at them.

I barely felt the cold seeping into my bones. I was drenched from top to toe, blinking furiously to get the water out of my eyes. If I didn't drown, I might die from sickness, the ghastly fever that often accompanied long stretches in the cold. I'd seen it take healthy seamen, making them waste away, racked by coughs.

Shouts drifted to me over the roaring of the sea. The men on the *Starlight* had seen me. One waved, his desperation clear even from the distance. Had they noticed that I was a woman yet?

By the time I finally got close enough to see them clearly, my entire body ached, my heart was beating faster than I thought possible and I was ready to give myself to the waves. Only Benjamin's voice kept me going.

Save them, Jonet.

Two of the seamen waved at me, the others busy trying to keep the ship afloat. I had to come aboard to guide them away from the cliffs and use the currents to carry them to safety, but if I got any closer, my little boat would be pushed against their much larger ship. I didn't want to lose my boat – but their lives were more important. If the deaths of my parents and Benjamin had taught me anything, it was that life was precious.

One of the men threw down a rope ladder. He shouted something, but the wind carried away his words. I pulled in one of the oars and used the other to turn the boat towards their ship until I was almost parallel. I'd only have one opportunity to reach for the ladder before the waves would carry my boat to its death. And me, if I didn't succeed.

I took a deep breath. I was trembling all over, both with fear and cold. This may be the most important moment of my life.

There was no time to think on it any longer. My boat

was in perfect position, so I stood, reached, jumped, clung to the ladder.

I let out a cry of triumph. I'd made it. I refused to look back to see my boat destroyed on the rocks and instead climbed up the ladder, my fingers stiff from the cold. The wet rope was rough and I felt my skin tear, but I didn't care.

Strong arms pulled me over the railing and held me until I stood on wobbly legs.

"How?" An old sailor stared at me from beneath bushy eyebrows.

"No time. I know how to get you out of here but you have to trust me."

"Captain-" the other man began but the old sailor simply looked at me, his eyes boring into mine. Time seemed to slow down as he appraised me.

"You know these waters?" he asked eventually.

I nodded. "My father was a fisherman."

There was no time to explain that he'd taken me along many times, that he'd taught me how to sail, that he'd gifted me my boat when I'd moved out from home. I may not be a fisherman like my father was, but he'd taught me enough to be confident.

"Help us," the sailor said simply.

His trust warmed me more than any fire could have. I staggered to the wheel. The lad clinging to it gave me a strange look but at a word from the captain he let me take his place. As soon as my hands touched the wood, a strange calm overcame me. I was in control. The ship bucked beneath me like a wild horse, tried to break free, but I kept hold of the wheel, leaning into it with the entire weight of my body.

As if I'd done this all my life, I shouted orders to the sailors. The captain repeated them in his much louder voice and everyone jumped to action. I could almost taste their renewed hope. They'd thought themselves lost but now they were fighting once again.

Slowly, we managed to turn the ship around, facing the waves. We couldn't sail straight away from the cliffs, there were rocks in the way, so I steered us slightly to the right, remembering the old maps my father had shown me. I could see them clearly in front of me, frayed at the edges, the currents and sandbanks marked, the rocks painted in red. From the grave, my father was helping me.

At some point, the captain took over, taking the wheel while I told him where to turn it. My arms were like jelly and I felt close to collapsing. Grateful for the reprieve, I took a step back – and the ship jerked to the right, waves crashed over us and icy water welcomed me into its deathly embrace.

Three

Tree Finnmen cam' fae der heem i' de sea

Fae de weary worm de folk tac free,

An' dey sall be paid wi' dc white monie!

— GAELIC INCANTATIONS, CHARMS
AND BLESSINGS OF THE HEBRIDES.
WILLIAM MACKENZIE, 1895

Hitting the water's surface was the worst pain I'd ever felt in my life. Sparks flashed in front of my closed eyes. I would have gasped and screamed if I hadn't been surrounded by water. Waves tossed from side to side. I didn't know what was up and what was down. My lungs started to burn with the need for air. I was drowning. Was that what Benjamin had felt? Had he given in to the sea and opened his mouth to take a final breath of saltwater?

I wasn't going to die today. Not here, not in the sea. I kicked my feet, trying to swim to the surface, wherever it may be, but my clothes were weighing me down. The current pushed me to the side, toying with me. The ocean was hungry and I was its meal.

I had to breathe. Air. I needed air. My lungs seemed to want to burst from my chest. I pressed my lips together as hard as I could, resisting the urge to breathe.

Something touched my leg. Seaweed? It clasped around my ankle and pulled. No, that wasn't seaweed. It was a hand. An iron grip that I couldn't escape, even when I kicked at it. I was too weak to fight. The ocean was beckoning.

Let me in. Breathe.

I could almost hear it call to me. I was so tired.

A hand wrapped around my right wrist. I didn't have the strength to even move my arm.

I was done.

I opened my mouth and swallowed the sea.

I breathed air. Gasping for breath, I coughed and sputtered the seawater that I'd swallowed. My eyes were swollen and everything was blurred. My body was numb, I didn't feel my arms and legs.

"Easy, take it slow."

A man's voice. I tried to see, but all I could make out where blurry shapes. I was no longer in the water. I could still hear it, the roaring of the storm-tossed ocean, but I was in a dry space. The ground beneath me was solid and didn't move, which meant I wasn't on a ship. Was I dead?

Was I about to meet the ferryman who would carry me into the afterlife?

A cough racked my body once again. My chest felt tight. I bet I had swallowed too much water. Breathing hurt. Surely that wasn't supposed to be the case? Unless I was in purgatory or hell. It could be some sort of torture. I'd always assumed I'd go to heaven, but maybe the people had been right and I had been wicked.

"You're safe now. Breathe."

A different voice, smoother than the first. Like milk and honey playing around his vocal cords while he was speaking. My vision was still too blurry, but I was starting to make out two figures close to me. Both seemed larger than they should be, but maybe it was because my vision was damaged.

"Who-" I broke into a coughing fit. My chest burned as if I'd swallowed half the sea.

"Don't try to speak." The first voice again. "Ma'vel, get her some whale milk. It'll soothe her throat."

Whale milk? And what kind of name was Ma'vel?

I rubbed my eyes. They were sore and puffy. Was any part of me not hurting? No, I was aching from top to bottom, even my toes. I wanted to curl up and cry.

A cool glass was pressed against my lips and I opened my mouth without thinking. The liquid was thick and tasted strangely sweet, reminding me of milk pudding. Just like the man had said, it instantly soothed my throat with every swallow. I greedily drank, realising just how thirsty I was.

"Take it slow," the second man, Ma'vel, said and took

away the glass. He sat down opposite me. "What's your name?"

"Jo...Jonet," I managed to croak. It still hurt, but at least I didn't erupt into another bout of coughing. "Where am I?" The oldest question in the book, yet the most important one.

"You're safe," the first male said softly. His voice was deep and melodious. "You were drowning and we fished you out of the sea. Sorry if I hurt your ankle."

I dimly remembered something grabbing my leg. That had been him? "I hope I didn't kick you."

"You did." He chuckled. "But don't worry, I've had worse. I'm Chiv, by the way. This is Ma'vel. And our brother Jamen is getting you some clothes as we speak. We need to get you out of the ones you're wearing."

What? They wanted me to undress?

I realised I was shivering. The pain had hidden the fact that I was freezing, but now that he'd made me aware of it, my teeth started chattering.

"I wish we could make a fire, but there's no dry wood in this cave," Ma'vel said, true regret reflecting in his voice. "We don't usually come here, but it was the closest place to take you. It's a pity humans can't breathe under water."

My heart missed a beat. *Humans*? As in, I was different because I was human? As in, they weren't human?

I rubbed my eyes again and slowly, my vision cleared. It was dark in the cave with only some light filtering in through gashes in the rock above us. I couldn't make out the facial features of the two men, but they certainly looked human to me. Two arms, two legs, a head each.

They were large, muscular, so tall that they would have stood out in a crowd, but... they had to be joking.

"What are you?" I asked. I couldn't believe I was actually posing that question.

"We are known as the finfolk," Ma'vel explained calmly, as if this was the most normal thing in the world. And as if he hadn't just brought every scary fairy tale I'd been told as a child to life.

The finfolk were evil sea-dwelling creatures who would sink ships, destroy fishing nets, strike bargains with fishermen and punish them severely if the sailors went back on their word. They were cunning, vengeful beings who you wouldn't want to cross. And they were a legend. Not reality. Before the people of Orkney had started blaming witches for their misfortune, missing ships, broken fishing lines and cracks in their vessels, they'd blamed them on the finfolk. To strike a deal with a finman was akin to making a bargain with the devil.

"You're making fun of me," I muttered.

The slapping sound of wet feet on stone made me turn around. I groaned when pain shot through my body. I had to be bruised all over. A third man walked towards me, his clothes tattered and hanging off him as rags. He resembled the other two in stature, with the muscular arms of someone used to hard physical work. His feet were bare. Long hair fell to his shoulders. He stopped right beneath a crack in the cave ceiling, letting a small sliver of light fall on his face. His features were strangely rough, as if a painter had used too large a brush. Even in the dark, it wasn't hard to see that the three men were related.

He held up a large bag, but it was too dark to see what it was. "I brought a blanket. It was all I could find."

Ma'vel huffed. "It'll have to be enough. Jonet, you better get out of these clothes. Do you need help?"

I turned back to him. They wanted me to undress. Here, in front of them. No woman with any decency would do that. Who did they take me for? Did they think I was a witch who slept with the devil, doing naked rituals under the light of the full moon?

"I'm not going to get naked," I said, but the croak in my voice turned it into a pitiful whisper rather than the confident statement I'd intended.

Chiv, the man with the deep voice, chuckled. "Humans are so precious."

"We can turn around," Ma'vel said in a much kinder tone. "I know how human women are obsessed with their modesty."

Obsessed? Modesty? I wanted to come up with some retort, but the words stuck in my throat when Chiv stepped forward, close enough for me to see more of him even in the dim cave. I gasped.

"Like what you see?" He chuckled again. "Ma'vel, give us some light."

Without warning, the cave turned bright as if the sun had suddenly appeared behind me. I turned around to see Ma'vel carry a ball of light in his hand.

"Magic," I gasped.

"Not quite, but I suppose that's what we shall call it," Chiv said with a wry smile at his brothers. It seemed like there was a hidden meaning in that smile, but I was too shocked to dwell on it.

"Magic," I repeated slowly, staring at the globe turning in Ma'vel's hand. It looked a bit like a glass ball with fire licking around its surface and was bright enough to light up the entire cave. I couldn't believe what I was seeing. But there was no other explanation. It had to be magic. Fire didn't burn in a ball and it certainly couldn't be carried on someone's palm.

Magic. Finmen. Finfolk.

It was real.

Now that Ma'vel was drenched in light, I got to see his entire body. What I'd thought were clothes were... I blinked. It looked as if sleek lengths of seaweed were stuck to his waist and shoulders. Did they glue them onto their skin instead of clothes? A few seaweed leaves hid his crotch from view, for which I was grateful. The rest of him was naked. Water pearled on his arms, glistening in the light. He almost seemed to sparkle. His long hair wasn't black as I'd first assumed, but dark green, the same colour as the seaweed protecting his modesty. I almost laughed myself. Here we were back to modesty.

I slowly turned to the other men, now fully illuminated by the ball of light. Their seaweed kilt and shoulder panels were almost identical to that of their brother - they'd said he was their brother, right? - although Chiv's waist seaweed was swept to the side a little, giving me a peek at his...

I averted my eyes. I'd never even seen Benjamin's manhood. I'd touched him through the thick fabric of his trousers while he'd slipped his hands beneath my shirt, but we'd never gone further than that. It had been hard to resist, but we'd been engaged to be married and I would have finally got to be with him fully on our wedding night.

I wished I'd gone against the rules. I would have been able to merge with him, become his for real. And now here I was, staring at these three beautifully built men. Heat flooded my cheeks. I shouldn't stare, not even with them being finfolk. Especially because they were finmen. They might take it the wrong way. I didn't want to get on the wrong side of them. If even half the stories were true... Drowning would have been a kinder death.

"Take a good look," Ma'vel said with a grin. "It's not like we haven't looked at you while you were unconscious. I've never seen a human female up close before."

My blush intensified. What did he mean, he'd looked at me? I still wore my clothes so at least he hadn't seen... For the first time since I'd awoken, I looked down at myself. I wanted to scream when I saw my shirt had ripped at the front, exposing one of my pale breasts. I hugged my arms around me chest, but it was too late. They'd already seen me. Who knew what they'd done while I'd been unconscious. Had they touched me? Had they-

"We didn't touch you," Chiv said surprisingly gently.

I gaped at him. "Did you read my mind? Can you do that?"

"It was written all across your face. But we're not like that. We don't take what isn't freely given. Besides, both Jamen and I have mates already. Ma'vel is the only one who hasn't found his yet.

Knowing that he was already married – at least that's

how I interpreted his talk of mates – made me feel better about being in the company of three unknown men. Chiv's gaze was fixed on my face and somehow, that calmed me a little. He wasn't staring at my chest. He may have looked out of curiosity, but then, so had I. I'd stared at the three men like I'd never looked at anyone before. If they hadn't been naked already, I'd have undressed them with my eyes.

I shouldn't think like that. When Benjamin had died, I'd promised to never have feelings for another man. He'd been my one true love. You only got to meet your soul mate once in your life. To hope for more was foolish and greedy.

"You should really get out of those wet clothes," Ma'vel said with a kind smile. "Humans are fragile. It would be sad if you'd die from the cold after we went through the trouble of saving you from drowning. You're very lucky we were in the area."

He exchanged a quick look with Jamen behind me and a strange expression flitted across his face. Was that guilt or did I misinterpret it?

"Was it you?" I asked before I could stop myself. "Did you attack the *Starlight*?"

Chiv kneeled in front of me so his face was level with mine. "We didn't *attack* them. They encroached upon our territory, then got in trouble. If they'd been somewhere else, we may have helped. Since they were fishing where they weren't supposed to, we decided not to intervene and let fate take its course."

Strangely enough, I believed him. He and his brothers didn't strike me as the violent finmen I'd been told about as a child. If they really were evil, they wouldn't have pulled me out of the sea, right?

The sound of my teeth chattering reminded me that I was slowly freezing to death. It was cold in the cave, although at least there was no draught.

"Can you turn around?" I asked shily.

Ma'vel smiled at me. "If you want us to. But if you want me to watch, I'd be happy to."

"Why would I want you to watch?"

He grinned. "I forget how prude humans can be."

"I'm not prude." Yes, I was. Especially compared to them. They didn't seem to care that most of their bodies were on display. Perhaps if I'd been as stunning as them, I wouldn't have felt as shy.

"Brothers, turn," Ma'vel commanded. To my surprise, the others did as he said without question. I'd taken Chiv for the most dominant of the three, but turned out I'd been wrong. With the way Ma'vel spoke, it was clear he was used to giving commands.

He handed me the bag before turning around himself, presenting me with his naked back. Only a few seaweed tangles were attached here, leaving most of his behind on full display. I forced myself to look away. Ogling a finman was asking for trouble.

In the bag was a thick woollen blanket. I had no idea how Ma'vel had got it here without it getting wet, but I didn't care. Checking one last time that none of the men were peeking, I peeled my soaked clothes off my skin. My muscles ached with every movement, but I had to be quick before the finmen got impatient. When I got to my underclothes, I hesitated. I should really take it all off to stave off the cold, but I was surrounded by three strangers, three *finmen*. Since my breasts were small and firm, I didn't wear a breastband, but I did wear linen drawers that now stuck to my skin, showing more than they hid. I grit my teeth and took off my drawers before wrapping the blanket around me as fast as possible. It was large enough to work as a dress that reached to my ankles while leaving my shoulders exposed. What I would have given for my shawl to wrap around my shoulders, but that had been lost to the ocean.

I was still shivering, but I could already feel the cold being drawn out of my body. A fire would have been ideal. Did Ma'vel's ball of light give off heat?

"You can turn around," I said quietly, shyness taking over. The blanket hid more than my wet clothes had, but I'd never exposed my shoulders to a man before, let alone three.

"That's better," Ma'vel said with an approving smile. "Now what are we going to do with you?"

Four

Sometimes about this Country, are seen these men they call Finn-men. In the year 1682, one was seen in his little Boat, at the South end of the Isle of Eda, most of the people of the Isle flock'd to see him, and when they adventur'd to put out a Boat with Men to see if they could apprehend him, he presently fled away most swiftly. And in the year 1684, another was seen from Westra.

— AN ACCOUNT OF THE ISLANDS OF
ORKNEY, JAMES WALLACE, 1688

I stared at him in shock. Was there any question about that? I wanted to go home, of course. What was he considering? Where they planning to take me to Finfolkaheem, the mythical city at the bottom of the sea? Or to Hildaland, the island they lived on during the summer, an island that wasn't on any maps and few had ever found?

"Please, take me back," I begged. "My betrothed will be waiting for me."

"Your betrothed? What's that?" Jamen asked, his brow furrowed.

"When a man proposes to a woman, they become betrotheds until the wedding," I explained. "We are to be married."

It hurt to say that. I was speaking words from the past. A year ago, it would have been true. Now, the lie was bitter on my tongue.

"Married," Chiv repeated. "I suppose we will have to return you to your betrothed then."

Ma'vel stepped forward and put a finger under my chin, forcing me to look up at him. "Are you happy?"

I blinked, taken aback. "Happy?" I croaked, my throat suddenly very dry again.

"It's a simple enough question. Are you happy?"

I'd already lied to them, so what bad would one more lie do? But from the way he looked at me, his eyes boring into mine, that strangely soft expression on his inhuman face...

"I don't know," I whispered.

Ma'vel stroked my cheek and I found myself leaning into his gentle touch. Nobody had touched me like that since Benjamin. And his hands had been rougher, nowhere near as soft and tender as this. My eyes burned, but this time it wasn't the sea's saltwater. A tear escaped, flowing down my cheek until it hit Ma'vel's fingers.

"I knew it," he muttered, still keeping his gaze fixed on me. I couldn't look away. Couldn't step back, away from his touch. He'd enchanted me, that had to be it. Finmen had magic, Jamen had shown that. It was the only explanation why I was reacting to him as I did. Why I wanted him to embrace me, press me against his chest. Why heat was blooming in my stomach, warming me from the inside.

My eyes fluttered shut and another tear broke free.

"You should come with us," Ma'vel said gently. "I felt your anguish as soon as you woke up. You're not happy among the humans. When you mentioned your betrothed, you turned even sadder."

"We can't let her go," Jamen sighed. "Females need to be protected. She's clearly not safe on her island."

"I'm safe," I protested, opening my eyes again. "And I need to go home. Thank you for saving my life, but I need to return. Please, take me home. Or at least to my boat if it's still seaworthy."

"It's not," Chiv said darkly. "It crashed against the cliffs, just like you would have if we hadn't dragged you out of the water. You owe us."

The warmth growing in my chest instantly dissipated and I finally stepped away from Ma'vel. I hated that Chiv was right. I did owe them. Would they collect my debt? Would they turn me into a slave like finmen sometimes did in the stories? The only thing that could turn a finman's mind was silver, but I didn't have any.

"I'll give you whatever you want, just let me go," I begged. "Please, don't hurt me."

The moment those words tumbled from my lips, I knew I'd made a mistake. Their expressions conveyed a mixture of hurt, anger and disappointment. Yet I still wasn't scared. I realised that now. I wasn't scared of them. I should have been, but I wasn't. On the contrary. I felt safe in their company. It had been nothing but a reflex to ask them not to hurt me. Something I thought was expected of me in this situation. A woman shouldn't feel safe when confronted with three mostly-naked men, right? But I did.

Ma'vel looked the saddest of the three. He sighed, then nodded to himself. "We'll take you home, if that's what you want. We'd never keep you here against your will. But I felt your anguish. I don't want you to feel that way. Nobody should have to."

My heart broke a little. I wished he was human. I wished I'd met him on Westray.

"I need to go," I whispered. "Please."

Ma'vel took my hand. "Then that's what we will do. We'll have to swim to get from the cave to your island. Hand Jamen your blanket, he'll make sure it won't get wet."

They were asking me to get naked again. My gaze fell on the pile of discarded clothes and I breathed a sigh of relief. If I was going to get wet again, I could put on some of my already drenched clothes. It wouldn't matter. And as soon as I was home, I'd light a fire and warm myself with a nice hot soup followed by a long bath. Yes, that was exactly what I was going to do.

I slipped into my shift and drawers, using the blanket as a curtain to shield me from their eyes. I wouldn't have needed to. They dutifully turned around without me even having to ask them. Impressive. I couldn't help but steel some glances at their half-naked bodies. Chiv was standing closest to me. His algae bands were stuck so tightly to his skin that they almost looked as if they were part of him. That couldn't be, right? They were just clothes and not... appendages or whatever you'd call them.

"Are they clothes?" I asked as soon as I'd dressed.

"Clothes?" Jamen looked at me with confusion. "Yes, you're wearing clothes now. Did you hit your head?"

"I mean the seaweed you have around your waist and on your shoulders. Do you wear them for decoration? Does every finman wear them in the same way?"

"Oh, you're talking about our greenskin?" Ma'vel took one of the algae strands attached to his hip bone and held it out to me. "Touch it."

I gingerly ran my fingers over it. It was warm and dry, not at all like I'd imagined.

Ma'vel groaned suddenly and threw his head back. "That feels good. Don't stop."

I stared at the green band in my hand. He felt that? I stroked it again with two fingers and was rewarded with something that could only be described as a moan. Embarrassed, I let go of it. I'd touched *him*. These seaweed strands weren't decoration, they were part of him. Of them all. And here I'd thought their bodies were human.

"Can you move them?" I asked.

Chiv shook his head. "Only in the water. They help with feeling the currents and choosing the best route. They also make us faster swimmers. But we can't move them like octopus tentacles, if that's what you were hoping."

"Not hoping," I muttered.

Jamen grinned. "Usually, we don't let anyone else touch them. Only our finwife gets to caress them. Ma'vel just showed you why." He laughed. "Although he showed remarkable self-restraint. If you'd been stroking my greenskin, I would have been on my knees. If I didn't have a mate already, obviously."

Embarrassment made me hug my blanket tighter to my chest. I'd touched Ma'vel in an intimate way without even knowing. I'd never touched a man inappropriately. I'd never even made Benjamin groan in that way. Ma'vel's sounds had been primal. They still echoed within my mind and the uncouth side of me wanted to hear him groan like that again and again.

"I need to go," I said before I could think of how wonderful it had felt to touch his greenskin and how much I wanted to stroke that of the others. I wasn't a harlot; I shouldn't be thinking that. It would be best to get as far away as possible from the finmen before I did something I'd later regret.

They all looked as if they wanted to stop me, argue with me, but none of them said a word. They led me to the mouth of the cave and I got to see where I was for the first time. I gasped and almost let my blanket drop to the floor. I'd assumed the cave was in a cliff near where the *Starlight* had been, but no. We were underwater. A thin film that looked like wobbly glass protected us from the ocean.

"How?" I stammered.

"Magic," Ma'vel said, sounding strangely choked.

"But there was light coming in from above! How is that possible? How deep underwater are we?"

"So many questions," Chiv chuckled. "To answer them all, we'd need more time. Maybe you should stay with us after all."

I pressed my lips shut. The temptation was strong, but no. I couldn't.

"Please, take me home," I whispered without looking at them. "Please."

Jamen came to stand by my side. "We're going to swim as fast as we can to the surface, but take a few deep breaths now. It's a long way up. Hand me your blanket, I'll keep it dry."

I did as he asked, soaking in as much air as I could, filling my lungs. I was a good swimmer but I was still hurting all over and exhausted. While he wrapped my blanket into the bag that had kept it dry on his way to the cave, Ma'vel and Chiv took me by the elbow, leading me to the barrier.

"Ready?" Ma'vel asked.

I took another deep breath and nodded. "Take me home."

The beach was deserted. I didn't know how the finmen had known that this was the closest beach to my house, but I didn't ask.

We stepped out of the water, Ma'vel and Chiv still holding me, steadying me. Even though they'd done most of the swimming and had simply pulled me along, this had been the last drop in the bucket of exhaustion. I was so tired that my legs were close to giving in. All I wanted was my bed. If it hadn't been raining, I may have simply laid down on the beach to sleep here. The storm had passed on, but dark grey clouds still hung low, mirroring my mood.

I didn't want them to go, but there was no other way. I took one last look at the three finmen, their imposing statures, their inhuman yet terribly attractive faces, their greenskin that was begging to be touched.

"Thank you again for saving my life," I said while wrapping myself in the blanket Jamen had handed me. "I will never forget you."

"As will we." Ma'vel bowed his head, suddenly strangely formal. "You're special, little human. It's been an honour to meet you."

He whistled and it didn't take long for a bright blue fish to appear in the water. It was unlike any fish I'd ever seen before and I was the daughter of a fishermen. I knew what creatures lived in these waters and this wasn't one of them. The fish turned its head and looked at me with a strange intelligence that reminded me of a cat staring at its prey.

"This is Fin," he introduced the fish. "She'll come with you. If you're ever in trouble or if you change your mind and want to stay with us after all, tell her and she'll know where to find us. You don't have to feed her, she'll find her own food, but she loves scratches between her ears."

"Ears?" I echoed, staring at the fish in front of me. "And how am I supposed to take her with me? It's not like I have a bucket of water to carry her in."

Ma'vel laughed. "Don't worry, Fin will walk. Come on, beautiful, don't tease the human. Shift."

Don't tease the human?! I was about to tell him exactly what I thought of that statement when the fish's scales began to glow bright blue before turning into fur. It all went so quick, it was hard to see whether they simply transformed into black fur or whether they disappeared and fur grew in their place, but within seconds, the fish was no longer a fish.

Meow!

A black cat looked up at me with an expression I could only call cheeky. Her eyes still showed the same intelligence, but they'd changed to the colour of her blue scales. She purred and rubbed against my naked legs. I couldn't help but reach down and pet her.

"This is your last chance," Chiv said, sadness reflecting in his voice. "Please, don't stay here where you're unhappy. Nothing good will come of it."

"It's my home," I muttered, fighting the impulse to tell them that I'd changed my mind. What was I doing? He was right, I wasn't happy here. But maybe that would change now that I'd saved the crew of the *Starlight*. People would see that I wasn't a witch. The seamen would be able to attest that I hadn't used magic to bring them to safety. It had been nothing but courage and local knowledge. The sailors on the beach could have done the same thing if they'd been brave enough.

Yes, things might change. I had to believe that. I had to think positive.

I looked at the three finmen one more time. "Goodbye. And thank you for everything."

Then I turned around before they saw the tears glistening in my eyes and walked away, through the machair and onto the path that led to my home.

Five

"Many a time has the Cathedral echoed with the screams and imprecations of reluctant women and men on their way, short as it was, to the dreaded Marwick's Hole."

— KIRKWALL IN THE ORKNEYS, B. H. HOSSACK, 1900

ONE YEAR LATER: 12TH NOVEMBER 1629, 3AM

A cat meowed above my cell. There was no doubt in my mind that it was Fin; I'd have recognised that meow anywhere. How had she got in here? No, how had she got from Westray to the Mainland?

I slowly got to my feet, fighting vertigo. Instead of a last meal like I'd hoped, my jailor had given me nothing but a beaker of stale water. He hadn't seemed to care if I collapsed on the way to my execution. Maybe it was best that way. Being unconscious while they strangled me sounded better than being awake during it. Killing me before burning my dead body at the stake was a small mercy. It could have been worse. I grimaced. Here I was, trying to think positive on the day of my execution. The next time I saw the sun would be the last time. Or was it raining? A storm, maybe? I thought I'd heard the wind howling last night, but the walls of the cathedral were thick and didn't let in much sound.

Fin meowed again.

"You don't want to come in here," I whispered. "There's no way out."

My cell was known as Marwick's Hole, but nobody had told me whether Marwick had been a prisoner like me or the architect of the dungeon. I'd been lowered into the chamber through a chute, the only way in or out. The hatch above me was open – I wasn't sure if that had been intentional or if my jailor had forgotten to close it - but there was no way for me to reach it. I had no chair or other furniture to use as a ladder. The cell was empty besides a thin layer of straw. I didn't even have a bucket and had been forced to relieve myself in a corner. Judging from the smell, the previous occupants of the Hole had done the same.

Fin's meow was more of an order than a plea. I sighed and stretched up my arms as far as I could. A ball of fur hit me and I barely managed to catch her. I squeezed her to my chest, soaking in her warmth.

Despite the dark, her eyes glinted blue, the colour of the scales she'd had as a fish.

"What are you doing here?" I whispered.

With a purr, she pressed her wet nose against my throat in a very familiar gesture. I was about to be executed and my cat demanded cuddles. I shouldn't be surprised. Cats were inherently self-obsessed, even if they could turn into a fish.

I scratched her between the ears. Her purrs grew louder, dispelling some of the darkness within me.

"Thanks for coming, little one. I don't know how, but I'm grateful."

"She didn't come alone." Ma'vel's familiar voice echoed from above. My heart skipped a beat. He'd come for me. Fin must have told them that I'd been arrested.

"We've got a rope," Chiv called. "Are you able to bind it around your waist or do you need me to come down and help you?"

As much as I wanted him down here simply for the comfort and safety his presence would provide, I didn't need him. I didn't know if there were guards going to come any second, so we had to be quick.

"I can do it."

They slowly lowered a rope down while Jamen provided a glowing ball of light that floated above the opening. I was going to ask him what other magic they could do later on, but right now, that wasn't a priority.

My fingers were cold and stiff, but after a few tries I managed to tie the rope around my waist. I picked up Fin again and called out for my rescuers to pull me up. As much as they tried to be slow and gentle, the rope cut into my belly and I had to stop myself from wincing in pain. Just like the first time I'd met them, I wasn't in the best shape. This time, I hadn't been close to drowning, but the people who'd brought me here from Westray hadn't been gentle. They'd been angry, full of hatred, and had let me feel their fury. I didn't want to think of the pain they'd inflicted on me. I was bruised all over even though I'd now been in Kirkwall for several days.

As soon as I was through the hole, I was pulled into a strong embrace. The fresh scent of the sea filled my nostrils and I breathed in deep for the first time since they'd taken me to the cathedral.

"So good to see you again," Ma'vel whispered into my ear. "We shouldn't have let you go." He sounded annoyed with himself.

As much as I should have protested, pushed him away, pretended to be modest, I just couldn't. I'd dreamed of him almost every night for the past year. He'd taken Benjamin's place in my dreams and I'd desperately hoped that one day, the dreams might become reality after all. Now, he was here, Ma'vel and his brothers, surrounding me like a protective wall. With them, I was safe.

"Let's get you out of here," the finman muttered, but he didn't let me go. He lifted me into his arms and carried me. I squealed before realising how good it felt. He was soft and warm and safe. I stopped squirming and leaned my head against his hard chest. Maybe he wasn't all that soft after all. Just like the first time I'd met them, they were wearing nothing but seaweed kilts. Ma'vel's chest was smooth, not a hair in sight. I supposed that was better for swimming. Before our annual swimming competition, the men would shave their bodies and smear themselves with oil to improve their speed.

When we reached the large doors of the cathedral, Ma'vel stopped and let the others go first. Jamen extinguished his ball of light and peeked outside, making sure the coast was clear. "Go," he whispered and opened the doors just wide enough for us to squeeze through.

"I can walk," I muttered, wanting to make it easier for Ma'vel. I wasn't small nor was I particularly thin, yet he carried me as if I weighed nothing more than a child.

"I know you can. But I don't want you to. It feels perfect, carrying you like this. Like it was always meant to be."

His words touched something deep within me. I would have cried if I hadn't already shed all my tears in the Hole.

"Hurry," Jamen admonished him. "The sun will rise soon and we still have a way to go."

"Where are you taking me?"

"Home," Chiv said simply. "And this time, we're not taking no for an answer."

I smiled. "I'm not going to say no."

"Good." Ma'vel pressed a kiss on my forehead. My face erupted into flames and I stared at him with wide eyes. He'd kissed me as if it was the most natural thing to do. Kissed me. His lips on my skin. The place where his lips had touched me was still tingling even though he was already on the move again, carrying me through the dark streets of Kirkwall. Jamen went ahead, making sure nobody was around, while Chiv took up the rear, watching for anyone who might be following us.

"Were there no guards?" I asked after a while.

Chiv chuckled. "There were, two of them, but they

celebrated the outcome of your trial with some rather strong whisky. They're out for the count. Serves them right."

I agreed with the finman. Celebrating my pending execution, that was sick. Not that I'd expected anything else. Nobody had shown me any kindness here in Kirkwall. They'd all wanted to see me burn, ignoring the fact that I was innocent. I was sure that even if there had been no accusations, no witnesses to speak out against me, I would have still ended up convicted to die. The crowd and the judge had been hungry for blood. There had been no other possible outcome.

They were more wicked than I could have ever been.

When we finally reached the harbour, I breathed in deep. A cool breeze swept away the smell of the dungeon that had still clung to me. I couldn't wait to wash off the dirt and grime and put on some clean clothes again.

Ma'vel stopped in front of a small boat, just big enough for the four of us to squeeze into. It had no mast and no oars.

Jamen and Chiv jumped down and then reached up, taking me from Ma'vel. I was tempted to tell them that I was very much able to climb into the boat myself, but I didn't have the energy. They were so gentle with me, treating me like I was special. After all the abuse of the last few days - no, months and years - I couldn't tell them to stop. I craved their company and their protection.

I ended up squeezed between Chiv and Ma'vel, while Jamen stood at the helm. I leaned against Ma'vel's legs, sighing in content. I was safe now.

Jamen began to hum an unearthly melody that was

unlike anything I'd ever heard. I closed my eyes, feeling the boat move through the waves faster than it would have with a sail. Magic.

The melody wrapped itself around me like a warm blanket and I let it lull me to sleep, safe in the awareness that the men would protect me from whatever threat would face us next.

Six

"Our skin-sewed Fin-boats lightly swim,
 Over the sea like wind they skim.
 Our ships are built without a nail;
 Few ships like ours can row or sail."

— HEIMSKRINGLA

I woke to the sound of waves crashing against rocks. For a moment, I didn't know where I was, until soft lips brushed my forehead.

"Welcome home."

Before I knew what was happening, I was lifted out of the boat. I blinked up at Ma'vel. A smile played around his lips as he looked at me.

"We're home."

He carried me up a narrow path winding its way up the cliffs and I was glad I was being carried. I was still feeling weak from not having eaten in too long and climbing this precarious path wouldn't have been a good idea.

"Where are we?" I asked.

"A small island we discovered a while ago. There's an abandoned cottage that I rebuilt during the past few months in the hope that it would one day become my home... our home."

I didn't know what to say to that. He'd rebuilt a house for me without knowing if we'd ever see each other again. That meant he'd been thinking of me as much as I had of him. Even though I'd only met him once - crazy to think that - I felt like I'd known him all my life. He resonated with my soul, as silly as that sounded. I wasn't scared in his presence. Wasn't scared at the prospect of spending the rest of my life with him. And I wasn't scared of replacing Benjamin with Ma'vel. It had taken me a long time to get over his loss and he would always be in my heart, but I had to move on. And if I was honest with myself, what I'd had with Benjamin hadn't been anything like what I felt when I was around the finman.

"Here we are."

I pulled myself from my thoughts and realised we'd made it to the top of the cliffs. Rolling green hills spread out in front of us. It didn't look all that different from Westray except that the colours were somehow more vivid. I turned around as much as I could in Ma'vel's arms. Beyond the cliffs, a thick fog hid the rest of the world from view. That matched the stories I'd heard about Hildaland, the magical home of the finfolk. An island hidden in the mists, surrounded by strong currents that would stop any ship from getting close. Only the magically steered boats of the finmen could push through the currents and the fog.

If Hildaland was real, what other legends would be true? I had so many questions to ask my finman. I smiled when I realised I'd thought of him as mine.

"That's your cottage over there." Chiv pointed at a large white house nestled beneath the closest hill. "We've prepared it for your arrival, but let us know if you need anything or want to change something. We didn't know what colours you'd like for your room but-"

"Stop talking," Ma'vel growled. "I'm sure she'll like it."

He and increased his pace, overtaking his brothers. In no time at all, we stood in front of the cottage, even larger than it had looked from a distance. A small well-kept garden surrounded it on both sides. Flowers I'd never seen before grew next to the green door, giving off a sweet fragrance that mixed with the salty sea air. But the most curious thing of all were the seashells that covered the walls. I'd thought the cottage had been painted white but it turned out the colour stemmed from the shells that covered every inch. I couldn't even see the original stone underneath. It was beautiful.

"Did you add them?" I asked, not able to take my eyes off the shimmering shells.

"I did," Ma'vel said, pride reflecting in his voice. "We made it large enough to have space for my future bride, but your room has been empty for a long time."

My room. Wasn't I going to share one with him? Maybe it was better this way. I didn't want to appear promiscuous. What would my father say if he saw me moving in with a man that I barely knew? He would have turned in his grave if he'd known I was about to share a house with a man I wasn't at least engaged to. Only one way to change that.

"Would you like to marry me?" I blurted. I clasped my hands over my mouth, unable to believe what I'd just said. My face grew hot and I wanted the ground to swallow me. Had I just destroyed it all?

Ma'vel gently set me to my feet, but I was too embarrassed to look at him, let alone the others. Oh God, what had I done?

"Marrying is a human custom," Ma'vel said. To my relief, he sounded neither angry not like he was making fun of me. "But if it will make you feel better, then yes, why not."

"Why do you want to marry?" Chiv asked, sounding genuinely curious. "Is it a human necessity?"

I forced myself to lift my gaze. The three of them gave an imposing sight and I almost looked away again.

"There are rules," I muttered. "A woman shouldn't live with a man she isn't wed to. I know it's not the same for you, but... I..."

"Will you marry me?" Ma'vel asked before I could dig my hole even deeper. "Jonet Forsyth, will you become my finwife?"

A strange heat bloomed in my chest. Love. Was that it? Yes. I loved him. As strange and magical as it was. The year apart had turned the seed of our first encounter into fragrant blossoms. "Yes," I breathed. "I do."

I didn't know what to do with myself, with my

hands, with everything. Was I supposed to hug him like my heart was begging me to? Kiss him? Or simply let my emotions take over and faint? I'd never felt this *much* at once.

"Humans use rings, aye?" Ma'vel asked, while already plucking two shells from the cottage wall. A light erupted from his fingers and before I could even see what he was doing, two smooth white rings lay on his palm. Magic, again.

"Am I allowed to kiss you before the wedding?"

Yes! I wanted to scream. But I wasn't a harlot. Maybe people in Kirkwall would do such a thing, but girls in Westray knew what was proper.

"No," I managed to say. "But there is no reason to wait with the wedding. I no longer have family who'd want to attend. I have no friends. Not anymore." That's when I realised one important thing. "We don't have a priest!"

Jamen cocked his head. "That's one of your pagan leaders?"

"They're men of God," I corrected.

"Your God isn't ours. From our view, you're pagans."

I realised he was right. To any Christian man or woman, they were heathens, but seen from their perspective, we were the ones with a different religion. Pagans.

"I'm sure God won't mind if we don't have a priest," I said after a moment. "It's the thought that counts, right?"

Ma'vel nodded. "I know how it's done. I've watched a human wedding before."

I looked at him, his naked body, his barely hidden

manhood beneath the greenskin. "Wouldn't you have stood out like a crab in a basket of cod?"

"I put on *clothes*," he said with distaste. "Dreadful things. My skin was sore for days after. But sometimes, we're sent to the human islands to see what's happening. Our leaders like to be informed of what the humans are up to and whether they could pose a threat to us."

I very much doubted that we could ever be a threat to beings able to wield magic, but I didn't say anything.

"Hold out your hand," Ma'vel said, his voice suddenly soft. I did as he'd asked and he gently took my wrist. "With this ring, I thee wed."

He slid the smallest shell ring onto my finger. It fit perfectly. Tears burned in my eyes as I looked at my hand. I'd been so close to wearing a ring once before. Now, it had finally come true.

Ma'vel handed me the other rings before holding out his left hand.

Slowly, very slowly, I slid the ring on his finger. Again, it was a perfect fit. He looked at his ring in wonder, seeming just as overwhelmed as I felt.

Ma'vel caught my hand. "We're married. Does that mean I can finally kiss you now?"

I no longer knew how to speak. I nodded and before I could even move, he'd pulled me into his arms and his lips found mine. My eyes fluttered shut. His hands caressed my face while he made me feel things I didn't think possible. Tingles ran all over my body, followed by the feeling of sunshine warming my skin. Heat pooled in my belly, a flame ready to be turned into an inferno. When I opened my mouth to gasp, Ma'vel used that opportunity to gently push his tongue past my lips. I'd never seen anyone kiss like that, but it felt too good to worry.

He wrapped me into his arms, making me feel safe, protecting me from the outside world. This was a fairy tale come true. We were on an island only found in myths and why shouldn't our love be the stuff of legends? I let go of all my innate inhibitions and did what my instincts commanded me to. I flicked my tongue against his. Ma'vel groaned and clasped his hands around my head, holding me in place while he began to ravish my mouth. This was no longer a gentle, chaste kissing. This was a claiming. He tasted of the sea and of freedom. I could drown in him without ever wanting to resurface again.

I let him plunder my mouth, clinging to him, never wanting this moment to end. We kissed and kissed until I was so out of breath I was starting to feel faint. Ma'vel seemed to notice and leaned back, giving me space to breathe.

"My wife," he whispered before pressing a row of kisses on my shoulder. "My finwife."

Happiness and love flooded me. Our kisses, his touches, his words... I'd never been so happy.

When Ma'vel and I finally broke apart, my lips were swollen and throbbing.

I sought the other two, half expecting them to be watching us, but they'd retreated into the cottage. Later, we'd celebrate with them. Now, I wanted to spend more time with my new husband. Get to know him inside and out.

A loud meow broke the spell. Fin rubbed against my legs. The third member of our family. And there would be more, I could feel it in the salty sea air tousling my hair. We were going to be a family now and forever.

I held out my hands to my husband. "Let's go inside."

And so we stepped into our new home, as finwife and finman, together. From now on, life was going to be good.

Seven

Fin had curled up on the sofa and was snoring softly. The living room of the cottage was extremely comfortable, much airier and bigger than my own little house. Square windows let in light, the glass not stained by ash and soot like I was used to. The furniture was very different from the wooden, simple chairs and table I had at home. The frames were made from sea-bleached driftwood while the base and pillows were woven from something that looked like dried seaweed. It kind of looked like they'd brought the ocean into the cottage.

"Want to see the rest?" Ma'vel asked eagerly. It was clear he wanted to show off his home – no, our home. It was still all sinking in. I was married. A wife to my husband. So much had happened in this one day. Instead of being burned at the stake like I'd expected, I'd been saved by a finman. I was the luckiest woman alive, especially now that I was married to him. My lips still throbbed from our kisses. I couldn't wait to explore his body. Now that we were wed, there was nothing stopping us. Not that Ma'vel had any inhibitions; that had been all me. I knew that I'd slowly have to give up the conventions and rules I was used to, but I was going to do it one step at a time. First, I had to convince myself that this wasn't all just a dream.

Ma'vel led me into a small but well-equipped kitchen. I didn't recognise half of the appliances in there.

"What is that?" I asked, pointing at a cupboard with a metal door.

"It's to keep food cool," Ma'vel explained, resting his hand on the table. "It's operated by magic. That way, milk and cheese won't spoil as quickly."

I opened the cupboard and held out my hand. He was right, it was cold inside. "Magic," I muttered.

Ma'vel put a hand on my lower back. "You'll get used to it. Wait until you see the crockery-washer. You just put in the dishes and they will come out clean."

"You're messing with me."

He laughed. "I'm not. I'll show you later, once we actually have some dirty plates. It'll save us a lot of time."

"Us?" I repeated. "You're going to help with the housework?"

"Of course," Ma'vel said, his eyes glinting. "Is that different in humans?"

I laughed. "Yes, very much so. Wives are expected to do the housework while the men go out and earn money. Of course, women also work on the crofts, offer services like repairing clothes, so in the end, we often do more work than the men."

"That's ridiculous," he huffed. "I knew humans were different, but it always surprises me just how different. They haven't changed much since we first arrived—"

He stopped himself, then turned to me and took my hand. "Let's have a look at the bedroom. Just the two of us."

His smile turned suggestive and a blush rose to my cheeks. Were we going to consummate our marriage now? It wasn't evening yet, but I supposed it didn't matter. This was all different from a normal marriage. I didn't quite know what the consummation entailed, except that there might be a blood stain on the sheets tomorrow and I could end up pregnant. Women didn't talk about the details of what happened during their wedding nights. When Sarah, one of my closest childhood friends, got married, she'd told me that it had been nothing like the magical moment she'd imagined. It had been painful. She'd said that her husband had enjoyed the consummation, but she'd been glad when it had been over.

My excitement washed away.

"What?" Ma'vel asked. He must have been watching me closely to notice my change of mood. I'd always thought I was good at hiding my true emotions, but he could read me without trouble.

"Will it hurt?" I blurted.

"What will hurt?" he asked sharply, grabbing my shoulders and looking up and down my body as if to search for wounds. "Are you hurt?"

"I'm fine," I muttered. "Nothing hurts."

"Then what's going on?" Ma'vel asked, the pressure on my shoulders easing as he relaxed.

"I was... the wedding night... I've been told that it can hurt."

Ma'vel sucked in a sharp breath. He gently steered me out of the kitchen so we could have some privacy. In the corridor, he cupped my face ever so tenderly. "Whoever told you that clearly didn't know what they were talking about. I will make sure that you experience nothing but pleasure tonight. No pain, I promise. You're my treasure, my finwife, my everything. Nobody will ever hurt you, least of all I."

I felt silly. Maybe Sarah and her husband hadn't known what they were doing. They may have made a mistake which had caused her to be in pain.

I looked at my husband, the confidence in his gaze, then smiled. "I trust you."

Ma'vel groaned. "You don't know what you do to me. If this wasn't our first time, I'd take you right here, right now. Show you pleasure like you've never experienced. Like no human female has ever felt."

A pleasant shiver ran down my back. "Let's go to the bedroom," I croaked.

My husband grinned. "Your wish is my command. Come. I designed the mural; I hope you like it."

When we stepped into the bedroom, I couldn't help but gasp. The entire wall behind the bed as well as the ceiling were covered in shells, just like the outside of the cottage, but here they'd been painted and arranged to create a vast mosaic.

Above us, colourful fish swam in azure-blue water. Behind the bed, a large turtle lazily paddled through the ocean, surrounded by large swaths of seaweed that almost seemed to move in the current. It was so lifelike that I couldn't stop staring. How long had it taken him to create the mural? If he'd hand-painted every single shell, it must have taken many days. And he'd done it for me, for us.

I reached up, cupped Ma'vel's cheeks and pulled him down.

"I love it," I whispered before pressing my lips on his. For a moment, he seemed too surprised to move, but then he wrapped his arms around my waist and pulled me against his hard body. I gasped when he took over, ravishing my mouth in a kiss wilder than any before. He tasted of the ocean, of freedom, and I was happy to drift in this wave of stormy desire. Warmth spread through my belly and a tingling started between my legs. A strange need filled me, but I didn't know how to satisfy that need. It was like I was hungry for food that I'd never tasted before.

Ma'vel moved his hands down until they cupped my buttocks. He squeezed, stoking the fire of want inside of me. His hardness pressed against me and I knew I wanted him. I'd never been surer of anything in my life. I wanted him.

"Is it alright if I undress you?" Ma'vel whispered in my ear. His hot breath on my skin gave me goosebumps.

I remembered the first time he'd wanted to undress me, after he'd fished me out of the sea. Back then, he'd been a stranger and I'd made him turn around. Now, I couldn't imagine anything better than having him remove my clothes, one by one, until I was bare in front of him. I was his and I was eager to prove it.

"Yes," I breathed before Ma'vel claimed my lips once more. His tongue plundered my mouth while he continued to massage my buttocks. The need for more was getting almost unbearable.

Ma'vel slid his hands beneath my blouse. His hands were soft, nothing like Benjamin's calloused hands had been. I realised I was okay with thinking about Ben in this moment. He was part of my past and always would be, but I had moved on and that was alright. I was allowing myself to be with my husband without regrets, without shame.

Slowly, Ma'vel explored my belly before his thumbs slid into the waistband of my outer skirt. A shiver ran down my back. I needed him to hurry up before I burned up from inside.

By the time he'd pulled down my skirts, my legs were wobbly and I was squirming against him, desperate for the heat to be soothed. My core throbbed and wetness was spreading between my thighs.

When he broke the kiss, I used that as my chance to gasp, "Hurry up."

Ma'vel laughed softly. "So impatient, my finwife."

He stepped forward, grabbed the collar of my blouse in his large hands. "I'll buy you a new one," he murmured —before tearing it apart. Buttons flew through the air, bouncing on the wooden floor. He pushed the torn blouse down my arms, letting it carelessly drop to the ground. Now I wore nothing but my drawers. My nipples pebbled when cool air hit them – or maybe it was the desire I felt for the male standing so close.

Ma'vel went on his knees and before I knew what was

happening, he pressed tiny kisses on the space just beneath my belly button. I sucked in a breath when he started pulling down my drawers. He didn't stop kissing me, but he slowly moved downwards, all the way to where my skirts had left an imprint on my skin. His tongue lapped at my skin, teasing me, before he continued his journey.

"Keep your eyes closed," he whispered, suddenly close to my ear as he lifted me onto the bed. The sheets were cool and soft beneath my naked skin, much softer than any fabric I had at home. Was this silk, real silk? Or some finfolk fabric that I'd never even heard about?

His hands gently took my ankles and spread my legs. Again, a cool breeze kissed my skin, this time between my thighs. The air tasted salty, almost as if he had brought his ocean home into our cottage.

Then, his hand cupped that soft space between my legs. A pleasant shiver raced across my skin, pushing warmth into my core. I pushed up my hips into that touch, wanting more. My husband slipped a finger between my folds, rubbing that nub I'd experimented with in the dark of night. It felt so much better than when I'd touched it myself. I moaned just when he pushed the finger inside of me. It felt tight, like I was too small or he was too big, but not in a bad way. He rubbed my nub again and I couldn't help but buck my hips against him. More. Please.

"Patience," Ma'vel muttered, his voice husky. "Let me prepare you first."

He kissed my nipples before taking one into his mouth. He suckled, as if he was a baby, and a strange wave of bliss overcame me. I wanted to let go, let it carry me with it, but I wasn't quite ready yet.

His lips crashed against mine and I tasted him again. It was hard to focus on the kiss. I wanted to reciprocate, take an active role, but there were so many sensations. My nipples ached, harder than ever, and the way he worshipped them only made my need worse.

I felt fuller and it took me a moment to realise that a second finger had joined the first. Time was flowing in a strange way. Past was present, future was past. I was floating on an ocean of bliss, held aloft by the hands of the only man who mattered. His hands roamed my body, letting me know I was his. And I was. His, forever.

When my husband positioned himself at my entrance, time stood still. This was the moment I'd been scared of, but all that remained was desperate need to have him inside of me.

He pushed in slowly, letting me adjust to the girth that was so much bigger than the two fingers earlier. It hurt, but it was a pleasant pain, only one layer among all the sensations. His hands caressed my body, distracting me with kisses and gentle touches. He played me like an instrument, knowing exactly what I needed to create a song of moans and heavy breathing.

By the time he was fully inside me, the pain had been washed away. I wanted to tell him to move, to take me, but words were leaves on the water's surface, hard to grasp. He waited a bit longer, his thumb drawing circles on my nub, driving me crazy. Then, finally, he pulled out almost entirely before pushing back in. I screamed out, not from pain but from pure pleasure.

He held my shoulders, steadying me as he increased his pace. I knew he was holding back. I was both grateful and frustrated. He didn't want to hurt me, but I needed more, just a little bit more to drive me over the edge. I was so close. I didn't know what awaited me on the other side, but there was only one way to find out.

He squeezed my nipples at the same time as he thrust into me so deep that I finally shattered. A gurgling scream came from my throat as I rode the wave, falling apart before being put together again. My hands clawed at the sheets while he held me, whispering to me in a language I didn't understand. I'd never felt so loved.

When the last quivers ebbed away, I drifted off, safe in the knowledge that this was only the beginning.

Epilogue

Fin had curled up across my lap, purring like a little storm cloud, his fins twitching every so often in some fishy dream. The sea lay calm beyond the cottage, kissed golden by the rising sun. The world was still and perfect.

Ma'vel sat beside me on the driftwood bench, his arm draped lightly across my shoulders. His warmth seeped through the thin shift I had thrown on. He hadn't spoken for some time, simply watching the sky as if searching for something hidden between the clouds. Was he thinking about last night? Our first time together?

The warmth I felt at the thought had nothing to do with the morning sun.

At last he broke the silence. "You should know the truth about me."

I turned to him, heart quickening. "What truth?"

His jaw tightened. "We were not born of this sea. Not truly. My people came from the stars. We crash-landed here long before your kind told stories of finmen. Our vessel broke, and so we made the ocean our home. We learned to hide, to let your people believe in myths. But I remember what we were."

I blinked at him, struggling to fit the enormity of his words into my small, human mind. People from across the stars. Not just sea-folk but strangers from another world. Yet when I looked into his dark eyes, all I saw was the man who had saved me, who had held me through the night, who called me his finwife.

"Does it matter?" I whispered.

He let out a slow breath, relief softening his features. "Perhaps not. Yet you deserved to know. There may come a day when someone comes to rescue us. When the stars call to us once more. But I have decided already, Jonet." His fingers brushed my cheek with reverence. "Even if they come, even if they rebuild the ship, I will not leave. My place is here, with you. You are my home now."

Tears pricked my eyes. I leaned into his touch, Fin's steady weight grounding me as the sun edged higher, turning the sea to molten copper. Ma'vel bent and kissed me softly, a vow sealed not in ceremony but in the quiet certainty of morning.

Together we sat on the threshold of our new life, watching the horizon, the warmth of his lips lingering on mine. Whatever the future brought, he had chosen Earth.

He had chosen me.

Love Ma'vel? This story is only the beginning. Journey into present-day Scotland with **Fionn***, the first full book in the* Starlight Mermen *series. Meet the brooding finman whose heart longs for love just as fiercely as the tides, and discover a romance that will sweep you away.*

For all the latest releases, author updates and cat pictures, subscribe to my newsletter:
skyemackinnon.com/newsletter

<h1 style="text-align:center">Resources</h1>

You can read the full Jonet Forsyth trial report in 'Publications of the Folk-lore Society':

https://archive.org/details/publicationsoffo49folk/page/74/mode/2up

The Survey of Scottish Witchcraft is a database containing all people known to have been accused of witchcraft in early modern Scotland (including Jonet):

https://witches.hca.ed.ac.uk/

A lovely little tale of a human man abducted by finwoman, page 18ff:

https://archive.org/details/scottishantiquar07unse/page/18/mode/2up

The Starlight Universe

This book is part of the Starlight Universe, an entire galaxy filled with hunky aliens, exotic planets, and the human women ready to find love among the stars.

Starlight Highlanders Mail Order Brides

Alien Highlanders in kilts come to Earth in search of brides... and take them to planet Albya. Three m/f standalones full of humour, action and steamy romance. Part of the Intergalactic Dating Agency.

Starlight Vikings

Set on Earth and on the spaceship Valkyr, this trilogy of m/f standalones is all about hunky alien Vikings in need of females. Part of the Intergalactic Dating Agency.

Starlight Mermen

Hundreds of years ago, they crash-landed on Earth and gave rise to many of our legends. Now, they're back, desperate for female mates. Part of the Intergalactic Dating Agency.

The Intergalactic Guide to Humans

A humorous take on alien abductions, probing and other shenanigans. One reverse harem trilogy about clueless aliens and the human woman they abducted, followed by several standalone romances with various pairings (m/f, f/m/f and m/m). If you want light entertainment filled with unicorns, fabulous misunderstandings and unusual body parts, this is the series for you.

Starlight Monsters

These aliens are not your usual humanoids... they have claws, fangs, tails, scales, knotty dicks and will growl at you. Interconnected m/f standalones with lots of action, steam and fated mates.

About the Author

Skye MacKinnon is a Scottish romance author who was raised by elves in the mystical Highlands and calls the Loch Ness monster her friend. Her bestselling books weave together romance with action, suspense and whimsical humour, creating page-turners filled with strong heroines, alpha heroes and loveable monsters.

Whether she's writing about aliens in kilts, hunky Vikings or cat shifter assassins, Skye likes to put a new spin on familiar tropes. Some of her heroines don't have to choose, some fall in love with other women, and others get abducted by clueless aliens.

Skye lives with her bossy cat on the west coast of Scotland and uses the dramatic views from her office as an inspiration, no matter whether she writes fantasy, paranormal or science fiction romance. Until she gets abducted by aliens, that is.

Subscribe to her newsletter:
skyemackinnon.com/newsletter

Buy your books direct from the author

GET 20% OFF YOUR NEXT EBOOK OR AUDIOBOOK!

USE CODE BOOKWORMS AT SKYEMACKINNON.COM/SHOP

EBOOKS, AUDIOBOOKS, PRINT BOOKS, MERCHANDISE & MORE

Also By

Find all of Skye's books on her website, **skyemackinnon.com**, where you can also order signed paperbacks and swag.

Many of her books are available as audiobooks.

SCIENCE FICTION ROMANCE

Set in the Starlight Universe

- **Starlight Vikings** (sci-fi m/f romance)
- **Starlight Mermen** (sci-fi m/f romance)
- **Starlight Monsters** (sci-fi m/f romance)
- **Starlight Highlanders Mail Order Brides** (sci-fi m/f romance)
- **The Intergalactic Guide to Humans** (sci-fi romance with various pairings)

Set in other worlds

- **Between Rebels** (sci-fi reverse harem set in the Planet Athion shared world)
- **The Mars Diaries** (sci-fi reverse harem)
- **Aliens and Animals** (f/f sci-fi romance co-written with Arizona Tape)

PARANORMAL & FANTASY ROMANCE

- **Claiming Her Bears** (post-apocalyptic shifter reverse harem)
- **Daughter of Winter** (fantasy reverse harem)
- **Catnip Assassins** (urban fantasy reverse harem)
- **Infernal Descent** (paranormal reverse harem based on Dante's Inferno, co-written with Bea Paige)
- **Seven Wardens** (fantasy reverse harem co-written with Laura Greenwood)
- **The Lost Siren** (post-apocalyptic, paranormal reverse harem co-written with Liza Street)

OTHER SERIES

- **Academy of Time** (time travel academy standalones, reverse harem and m/f)
- **Defiance** (contemporary reverse harem with a hint of thriller/suspense)

STANDALONES

- Song of Souls – m/f fantasy romance, fairy tale retelling
- Highland Butterflies – sapphic romance
- Wings of Time and Fate - epic fantasy

BOX SETS

- Daggers & Destiny – a fantasy romance starter library
- Stars & Seduction - a science fiction romance starter library